BEATRIX POTTER'S
NURSERY RHYME BOOK

With new reproductions from the original illustrations

BY **BEATRIX POTTER**™

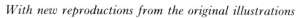

F. WARNE & CO.

Contents

Introduction

Beatrix Potter was very fond of rhymes. This book combines poems from the 1905 and 1917 *Appley Dapply* collections, rhymes from the *Cecily Parsley* collection, the Squirrel Nutkin riddles, rhymes from *The Tailor of Gloucester* and verses and jingles from some of the other tales, to make a book of some of Beatrix Potter's favourite nursery rhymes.

The old woman
who lived in a shoe

You know the old woman who lived in a shoe,
And had so many children she didn't know what to do?
She gave them some broth without any bread,
She whipped them all round and put them to bed.
I'm sure if she lived in a little shoe house,
That little old woman was surely a mouse!

The mouse's find

I found a tiny pair of gloves
    When Lucie'd been to tea,
They were the dearest little loves –
    I thought they'd do for me –

I tried them – (quite inside them!)
    They were *much* too big for me!
I wear gloves with one button-hole
    When *I* go out to tea.

I'll put them in an envelope
    With sealing wax above,
I'll send them back to Lucie –
    I'll send them with my love.

Goosey Goosey Gander

Goosey, goosey, gander,
  Wither will you wander?
Upstairs and downstairs
  And in my lady's chamber!

There I met an old man
  That would not say his prayers,
So I took him by the left leg
  And threw him down the stairs!

I went into my grandmother's garden

I went into my grandmother's garden,
  And there I found a farthing.
I went into my next door neighbour's,
  There I bought a pipkin and a popkin,
A slipkin and a slopkin,
A nailboard, a sailboard,
  And all for a farthing.

If acorn-cups were tea-cups

If acorn-cups were tea-cups,
  what should we have to drink?
Why! honey-dew for sugar,
  in a cuckoo-pint of milk;

With pats of witches' butter
  and a tansey cake, I think,
Laid out upon a toad-stool
  on a cloth of cob-web silk!

Cecily Parsley

Cecily Parsley lived in a pen,
And brewed good ale for gentlemen;

Gentlemen came every day,
Till Cecily Parsley ran away.

Gravy and potatoes

Gravy and potatoes
   In a good brown pot –
Put them in the oven,
   and serve them very hot!

Once I saw a little bird

Once I saw a little bird
   Come hop, hop, hop!
So I cried: 'Little bird,
   Will you stop, stop, stop?'

And was going to the window
   To say, 'How do you do?'
But he shook his little tail
   And away he flew.

This pig went to market

This pig went to market;
  This pig stayed at home;
This pig had a bit of meat;
  And this pig had none;
This little pig cried
  'Wee! wee! wee!
I can't find my way home.'

Hey diddle dinketty

Hey diddle dinketty, poppetty, pet!
The merchants of London they wear
    scarlet;
Silk in the collar, and gold in the hem,
So merrily march the merchantmen!

Sieve my lady's oatmeal

Sieve my lady's oatmeal,
Grind my lady's flour,
Put it in a chestnut,
Let it stand an hour –
One may rush, two may rush,
Come, my girls, walk under the bush.

Four-and-twenty tailors

Four-and-twenty tailors
Went to catch a snail,
The best man amongst them
Durst not touch her tail;
She put out her horns
Like a little kyloe cow,
Run, tailors, run!
Or she'll have you all e'en now!

12

I had a little nut-tree

I had a little nut-tree,
Nothing would it bear
But a golden nutmeg,
And a silver pear.

The King of Spain's daughter
Came to visit me,
And all for the sake of
My little nut-tree!

I skipp'd over water,
I danced over sea,
And all the birds in the
air couldn't catch me.

Buz, quoth the blue fly

Buz, quoth the blue fly;
  hum quoth the bee;
Buz and hum they cry,
  and so do we!

In his ear, in his nose,
  Thus do you see,
He ate the dormouse,
  Else it was thee.

Hitty Pitty

Hitty Pitty within the wall,
Hitty Pitty without the wall;
If you touch Hitty Pitty,
Hitty Pitty will bite you!

Answer: *A nettle*

Arthur O'Bower

Arthur O'Bower has broken his band,
He comes roaring up the land!
The King of Scots with all his power,
Cannot turn Arthur of the Bower!

Answer: *The wind*

Hickamore, Hackamore

Hickamore, Hackamore, on the King's
  kitchen door;
All the King's horses, and all the
  king's men,
Couldn't drive Hickamore, Hackamore,
Off the King's kitchen door.

Answer: *A sunbeam*

As I went over Tipple-tine

Hum-a-bum! buzz! buzz!
  Hum-a-bum buzz!
As I went over Tipple-tine
  I met a flock of bonny swine;

Some yellow-nacked, some yellow backed!
  They were the very bonniest swine
  That e'er went over Tipple-tine.

Answer: *Bees*

Humpty Dumpty
lies in a beck

Humpty Dumpty lies in the beck,
With a white counterpane round his neck,
Forty doctors and forty wrights,
Cannot put Humpty Dumpty to rights!

Answer: *An egg*

A house full, a hole full

A house full, a hole full!
And you cannot gather a bowl-full!

Answer: *Smoke*

Riddle me, riddle me,
rot-tot-tote

Riddle me, riddle me, rot-tot-tote!
A little wee man, in a red red coat!
A staff in his hand, and a stone in his throat;
If you'll tell me this riddle, I'll give you a groat.

Answer: *A red cherry*

16

Flour of England, fruit of Spain

Flour of England, fruit of Spain,
Met together in a shower of rain;
Put in a bag tied round with a string,
If you'll tell me this riddle,
I'll give you a ring!

Answer: *A plum pudding*

The man in the wilderness

The man in the wilderness said to me,
'How many strawberries grow in the
   sea?'
I answered him as I thought good –
'As many red herrings as grow in the
   wood.'

Tom, Tom the piper's son

Tom, Tom the piper's son,
  stole a pig and away he ran!
But all the tune that he could play,
  was 'Over the hills and far away!'

Tom wih his pipe made such a noise,
  He called up all the girls and boys –
And they all ran to hear him play
  'Over the hills and far away!'

A funny old mother pig

A funny old mother pig lived in a stye,
    and three little piggies had she;
'Ti idditty idditty, umph, umph, umph!'
    and the little pigs said, 'wee, wee, wee!'

Those three little piggies grew peaky and lean,
    and lean they might very well be;
For somehow they couldn't say 'umph, umph,umph!'
    and they wouldn't say 'wee, wee, wee!' –
For somehow they couldn't say 'umph, umph, umph!'
    and they wouldn't say 'wee, wee, wee!'

We have a little garden

We have a little garden,
  A garden of our own,
And every day we water there
  The seeds that we have sown.

We love our little garden,
  And tend it with such care,
You will not find a faded leaf
  Or blighted blossom there.

Pussy-cat sits
by the fire

Pussy-cat sits by the fire;
   How should she be fair?
In walks the little dog,
   Says 'Pussy! are you there?

'How do you do, Mistress Pussy?
   Mistress Pussy, how do you do?'
'I thank you kindly, little dog,
   I fare as well as you!'

Diggory Diggory Delvet

Diggory Diggory Delvet!
A little old man in black
    velvet;
He digs and he delves –
You can see for yourselves
The mounds dug by Diggory
    Delvet.

Babbity Bouster Bumble Bee

Babbity Bouster Bumble Bee!
    Fill up your honey bags, bring them to me!
Humming and sighing – with lazy wing
    Where are you flying – what song do you sing?

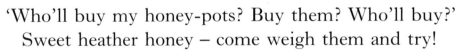

'Who'll buy my honey-pots? Buy them? Who'll buy?'
    Sweet heather honey – come weigh them and try!
– Honey-bag, honey-pot, home came she!
    Nobody buys from a big Bumble Bee!

There once was an amiable guinea-pig

There once was an amiable
   guinea-pig,
Who brushed back his hair like
   a periwig –

He wore a sweet tie
   As blue as the sky –

And his whiskers and
   buttons
Were very big.

Old Mr. Pricklepin

Old Mr. Pricklepin
  has never a cushion to
  stick his pins in,
His nose is black and his
  beard is grey,
And he lives in an ash stump
  over the way.

Tommy Tittle-mouse

I've heard that Tommy
  Tittle-mouse
Lived in a tiny little house,
Thatched with a roof of
  rushes brown
And lined with hay and
  thistle-down.

Walled with woven grass and
  moss,
Pegged down with willow
  twigs across.
Now wasn't that a charming
  house
For little Tommy
  Tittle-mouse?

Pig Robinson Crusoe

Poor Pig Robinson Crusoe!
Oh, how in the world could they do so?
They have set him afloat,
In a horrible boat,
Oh, poor Pig Robinson Crusoe!

When the dew falls silently

When the dew falls silently
   And stars begin to twinkle,
Underneath the hollow tree
   Peeps poor Tiggy-winkle.

Where the whispering waters pass –
   Her little cans twinkle,
Up and down the dewy grass
   Trots poor Tiggy-winkle.

Hey diddle diddle

Hey diddle diddle,
The cat and the fiddle,
The cow jumped over the moon;
The little dog laughed
To see such sport,
And the dish ran away
   with the spoon.

Mrs Tiggy-winkle's ironing song

Lily-white and clean, oh!
With little frills between, oh!
  Smooth and hot – red rusty spot
Never here be seen, oh!

Three blind mice

Three blind mice, three blind mice,
See how they run!
They all run after the farmer's wife,
And she cut off their tails with a
  carving knife,
Did you ever see such a thing in
  your life
As three blind mice!

Knitting

Knitting, knitting, 8, 9, 10,
  I knit socks for gentlemen;
I love muffin and I love tea;
  Knitting, knitting, 1, 2, 3!

Fishes come bite!

Fishes come bite!
Fishes come bite!
I have fished all day;
I will fish all night.
I sit in the rain on my lily-leaf boat,
But never a minnow will bob my float.
Fishes come bite!

Appley Dapply

Appley Dapply, a little
  brown mouse,
Goes to the cupboard in
  some-body's house.

In somebody's cupboard
  There's everything nice,
Cake, cheese, jam, biscuits,
– All charming for mice!

Appley Dapply has little
  sharp eyes,
And Appley Dapply is *so* fond
  of pies!

30

Little Poll Parrot

Little Poll Parrot
Sat in a garret
Eating toast and tea!
A little brown mouse
Jumped into his house,
And stole it all away!

Ladybird, ladybird, fly away home

Ladybird, ladybird,
  Fly away home,
Your house is on fire
  And your children all gone;
All except one
  And her name is Ann,
And she has crept under
  The pudding pan.

Three little mice sat down to spin

Three little mice sat down to spin,
Pussy passed by and she peeped in.
'What are you at, my fine little men?'

'Making coats for gentlemen.'
'Shall I come in and cut off your threads?'
'Oh, no! Miss Pussy, you'd bite off our heads!'

The little black rabbit

Now who is this knocking
  at Cottontail's door?
Tap tappit! Tap tappit!
  She's heard it before?

And when she peeps out
  there is nobody there,
But a present of carrots
  put down on the stair.

Hark! I hear it again!
  Tap, tap, tappit!
  Tap tappit!
Why – I really believe it's a
  little black rabbit!

To Market! To Market!

To Market! To Market!
  Now isn't this funny?
You've got a basket,
  and I've got some money!
– We went to market
  and I spent my money,
Home again! home again!
  Little Miss Bunny!

Ninny Nanny Netticoat

Ninny Nanny Netticoat,
In a white petticoat,
  With a red nose –
The longer she stands,
The shorter she grows.

Answer: *A candle*

I saw a ship a-sailing

I saw a ship a-sailing
A-sailing on the sea;
And Oh! it was all laden
With pretty things for thee!

There were comfits in the cabin
And apples in the hold;
The sails were made of silk
And the masts were made of gold.

And four and twenty sailors
That stood upon the decks
Were four and twenty white mice
With chains about their necks.

The captain was a guinea-pig –
The pilot was a rat –
And the passengers were rabbits
Who ran about, pit pat!

Tabitha Twitchit is grown so fine

Tabitha Twitchit
 is grown so fine
She lies in bed
 until half past nine.
She breakfasts on muffins,
 and eggs and ham,
And dines on red-herrings
 and rasp-berry jam!!

Hark! hark! the dogs do bark

Hark! hark!
 The dogs do bark,
The beggars are come to town,
 Some in tags
 And some in rags
And one in a velvet gown!

Kadiddle, kadiddle, kadiddle

Kadiddle,
  kadiddle, kadiddle!
Come dance to my
  dear little fiddle?
(Kadiddle,
  kadiddle, kadiddle,
Come dancing along
  down the middle...
Oh silly Kadiddle,
  Kadiddle!)

Old King Cole

Old King Cole was a merry old soul,
And a merry old soul was he,
He called for his pipe
  And he called for his bowl,
And he called for his fiddlers three –

Fiddle fiddle fiddle!
  Went the fiddlers three,
Fiddle, fiddle, fiddle, fiddle, fee!
Oh there's none so rare
  As can compare
With King Cole and his fiddlers three!

My little old man
and I fell out

My little old man and I fell out,
How shall we bring this matter about?
Bring it about as well as you can,
And get you gone, you little old man!

Ride a cock-horse

Ride a cock-horse to Banbury Cross
To see a fine lady upon a white horse;
Rings on her fingers and bells on her toes,
And she shall have music wherever she goes!

Publisher's Note

All the illustrations are by Beatrix Potter, taken from her tales and other works.

The reproductions in this book have been made using the most modern electronic scanning methods from entirely new transparencies of Beatrix Potter's original watercolours. They enable Beatrix Potter's skill as an artist to be appreciated as never before, not even during her own lifetime.

FREDERICK WARNE

Published by the Penguin Group
27 Wrights Lane, London W8 5TZ, England
Penguin Books USA Inc., 375 Hudson Street, New York, New York 10014, USA
Penguin Books Australia Ltd, Ringwood, Victoria, Australia
Penguin Books Canada Ltd, 10 Alcorn Avenue, Toronto, Ontario, Canada M4V 3B2
Penguin Books (NZ) Ltd, 182-190 Wairau Road, Auckland 10, New Zealand
Penguin Books Ltd, Registered Offices: Harmondsworth, Middlesex, England

This edition with new reproductions of Beatrix Potter's illustrations
first published 1995
Copyright © Frederick Warne & Co., 1995
New reproductions copyright © Frederick Warne & Co., 1993, 1995
Copyright in text and original illustrations © Frederick Warne & Co., 1903, 1905,
1910, 1911, 1913, 1917, 1922, 1930, 1984

1 3 5 7 9 10 8 6 4 2

Frederick Warne & Co., is the owner of all rights, copyrights and trademarks in the
Beatrix Potter character names and illustrations

ISBN 0 7232 4249 6

Colour reproduction by Saxon Photolitho, Norwich
Printed and bound in Great Britain by
William Clowes Limited, Beccles and London